An I Can Read Book®

THE KNOW-NOTHINGS

by Michele Sobel Spirn

pictures by R. W. Alley

HarperTrophy®

A Division of HarperCollins*Publishers*

To Steve and Josh, the Know-It-Alls
and to my parents, Jack and Sylvia Sobel
—M. S. S.

For Norma and Bob
—R. W. A.

Library of Congress Cataloging-in-Publication Data
Spirn, Michele.
The Know-Nothings / story by Michele Sobel Spirn ; pictures by R. W. Alley.
p. cm. — (An I can read book)
Summary: Four friends called the Know-Nothings, because they don't know very much, decide to make lunch.
ISBN 0-06-024499-2. — ISBN 0-06-024500-X (lib. bdg.)
ISBN 0-06-444226-8 (pbk.)
[1. Cookery—Fiction. 2. Humorous stories.] I. Alley, R. W. (Robert W.), ill. II. Title. III. Series.
PZ7.S757Kn 1995 93-43533
[E]—dc20 CIP
AC

❖

First Harper Trophy edition, 1997

CONTENTS

NORRIS
MORRIS
DORIS
BORIS

BORIS GETS LOST

Once there were four good friends.

Their names were Boris, Morris,

Doris, and Norris.

People called them Know-Nothings.

They didn't know much,

but they knew they liked each other.

One day the Know-Nothings
were very hungry.
Boris, Morris, Doris, and Norris
wanted to have lunch.

“I will cook,” said Doris,

“but first, I must find out

how many people will eat.”

Doris counted one, two,

three Know-Nothings.

"There are three of us," said Doris.

"I will make lunch for three."

"I always thought there were

four of us,"

said Boris.

"You are right,"

said Doris.

"There are four of us.

One of us must be missing!"

“Norris is missing,” said Morris.

“He went to visit his grandma.”

“No, I did not,” said Norris.

“I am here.”

"So you are," said Morris.

"It must be Boris.

Maybe he fell in the lake."

"We must save him!" Doris said.

"Oh, no!" cried Boris.

"There are sharks in the lake.

Hurry before they eat me."

"Boris!" cried Morris, Doris, and Norris. "You are here!"

"How did you get out of the lake?" Doris asked.

"It wasn't easy," said Boris.

"Ten big, mean sharks swam up.

I punched them in the nose and

swam away as fast as I could.

Now I am here."

"And you're not even wet,"

said Norris.

"What a hero you are!" cried Morris.

“Hooray for Boris!”
cried the Know-Nothings.
And they hugged Boris
as hard as they could.

THE KNOW-NOTHINGS MAKE LUNCH

"Now that we are all here,"

said Doris, "what shall I cook?"

"I like French fries,"

said Boris.

"No good," said Doris.

"Why not?" asked Morris.

“Everyone knows French fries
come from France,” said Doris.
“France is too far away.
I am hungry now.”

"Okay," said Norris.

"Let's have hamburgers."

"No good," said Boris.

"We don't have any ham."

"Look," said Morris.

"I found a box of noodles."

He shook it.

"They sound good," he said.

"Okay," said Boris. "Let's eat."

"These are a little hard,"

said Doris.

"They are crunchy," said Boris.

"We can make them softer,"

said Norris.

"How?"

asked Morris.

"Let's jump on them,"

said Norris.

Scrunch! Scrunch!

"They don't look any softer,"
said Boris.
"They don't feel any softer,"
said Doris.

"They are not soft at all!"

cried Norris.

"Now they are just crumbs!"

“I am still hungry,” said Morris.

“Me too,” said Doris.

“Here are some bananas,”

said Norris. “We can eat them.”

"They don't taste very good,"

said Doris.

"It must be those funny coats

they are wearing," said Morris.

"Maybe we should take off
their coats," said Boris.
"Oh, no," said Morris.
"Don't do that."
"Why not?" asked Doris.

"They will be cold
without their coats," said Morris.
"They will shake and shiver so much
we will never be able to eat them."
"Right," said the Know-Nothings.

The four Know-Nothings
looked at each other.
"No French fries," said Boris.
"No hamburgers," said Norris.
"No noodles," said Morris.
"No bananas," said Doris.
Boris, Morris, Doris, and Norris
stared at the table.
"I have an idea," said Norris.
"Let's wait for breakfast.
Everyone knows breakfast
is easy to make."

"What a good idea," said Doris.

"You are so clever," said Morris.

"You have saved the day,"

said Boris.

The Know-Nothings

put their napkins on their laps.

They held their forks in their hands

and waited for breakfast.

THE KNOW-NOTHINGS GET FED UP

It was a long wait for breakfast.

Boris, Morris, Doris, and Norris

were very hungry.

"I am tired of sitting," said Boris.

He walked around and around.

"Ah ha!" cried Boris, and ran inside.

"I have an idea!

Quick, Morris, get your drum!

Doris, get your French horn.

Norris, we need your flag.

Now I will need a stick,"

said Boris. "Wait here."

Soon Boris came back

with a long stick.

"Wave your flag, Norris.

Doris, play your horn.

Morris, bang your drum.

I will lead."

Boom! Boom!

Oompah! Oompah!

"Good," said Boris, "now do it again,

and walk very fast."

Boom! Boom! Boom!

Oompah!

Oompah!

Oompah!

"This is very nice,

but what are we doing?"

yelled Morris.

"We are marching," yelled Boris.

"Why?" asked Doris.

"Because everyone knows

time marches on.

We are helping time to march faster.

Then we can have breakfast,"

said Boris.

"Good idea," yelled Norris.

The Know-Nothings marched

faster and faster.

Soon their ears hurt.

Their feet were tired.

"Is it breakfast yet?"

asked Norris.

"Breakfast time is still not here,"

said Boris.

"I am fed up," said Doris.

"No, you're not," said Morris.

"You have not eaten anything.

You are as hungry as we are."

"Breakfast will never come,"

said Doris.

Norris, Morris, and Boris
began to cry.
"Don't cry," said Doris.
"I have an idea."
"What?" cried Morris, Boris,
and Norris.
"We tried lunch," said Doris.
"That was too hard.
We waited for breakfast.
It didn't come.
So let's get dinner.
We will go to France.

By the time we walk to France,

it will be dinnertime

and we can get French fries."

"What a great idea," said Morris.

"Three cheers for Doris,"

yelled Boris.

"We will get dinner!"

"Hooray!" shouted the Know-Nothings.

"We are going to France

for French fries!"

FRENCH DRESSING

The Know-Nothings got ready to go to France.

Doris put on a new hat.

"Why are you wearing that hat?"

asked Boris.

"This is my French hat,"

said Doris.

"I don't have a French hat,"

said Boris.

"What can I wear?

I want to look French."

Norris gave him a bottle.

"A bottle is not French," said Boris.

"Read the label," said Norris.

"It says 'French dressing,'"

said Boris.

Boris put the bottle on his head.

"I feel so French now," he said.

“I want to look French too,”

said Norris. “What can I wear?”

Doris gave him two pieces of toast.

“This is bread!” cried Norris.

“This is not French.”

"Of course it is," said Doris.

"Everyone knows about French toast."

"Of course," said Norris.

"Thank you, Doris.

You are so clever."

Norris put the toast on his head.

"What about me?" yelled Morris.

The Know-Nothings looked around.

Nothing looked French.

Morris was sad.

He wanted to look French.

“I know!” cried Norris.

He ran into the other room.

“Where did he go?” asked Doris.

Norris came back

with Doris’s French horn.

"Norris, you are so clever,"

said Doris.

"Morris, you must wear

the French horn.

You will look so French."

"Yes, I feel very French.

I am so happy," said Morris.

"Hooray!" cried the Know-Nothings.

"Now we are ready to go to France!"

The Know-Nothings walked and walked.

"Why are people looking at us?"

asked Norris.

"They think we look so French,"

said Doris.

"We are going to France," said Boris.

"We will get French fries."

Everybody laughed.

"Something smells good," said Morris.

"Something like French fries."

Doris sniffed.

"You are right, Morris," she said.

"We must be in France."

"Hooray!" cried the Know-Nothings.

FRANCE

They walked around the corner.

“Look!” cried Doris. “French fries!”

“Lots of French fries for us!”

yelled Norris.

“Mmm!” said Boris.

Morris could not talk.

His mouth was full.

The Know-Nothings gobbled
all their French fries.
"I thought France was far away,"
Boris said, "but it is very close."
"I thought France
would look different,"
said Doris,
"but it looks just like home."
"We have learned a lot today,"
said Morris.
"Yes," said Norris,
"and we got our French fries."
"We are all so clever," Doris said.

“Hooray for us!”
cried the Know-Nothings,
and they walked home happy
and full of French fries.